Shopkins™
Once you shop...You can't stop!

THE SECRET SHOPKIN

By Meredith Rusu

Published by Scholastic Inc., *Publishers since 1920*. SCHOLASTIC and associated logos are trademarks and/or registered trademarks of Scholastic Inc.

The publisher does not have any control over and does not assume any responsibility for author or third-party websites or their content.

This book is a work of fiction. Names, characters, places, and incidents are either the product of the author's imagination or are used fictitiously, and any resemblance to actual persons, living or dead, business establishments, events, or locales is entirely coincidental.

ISBN 978-1-338-03297-0

10 9 8 7 6 5 4 3 2   16 17 18 19 20

Printed in the U.S.A.   132

First printing 2016 • Book design by Erin McMahon

Scholastic Inc.

One bright and sunny-side up morning in Shopville, Suzie Sundae comes running up to her friends.

"Apple Blossom! Cheeky Chocolate!" she cries. "I have the latest scoop on the Secret Shopkin!"

"The secret who?" asks Cheeky.

"Oh my groceries," says Suzie. "It's only the juiciest gossip around the Small Mart! A mysterious masked hero has been helping Shoppies in need." "*Hmm.* Sounds a little off-the-shelf to me," says Cheeky.

"No, it's true!" insists Apple. "I saw him myself."
"You did?" Suzie gasps.
"Uh-huh," says Apple. "It happened just the other day."

"I was baby-sitting Dum Mee Mee. Suddenly, there was a can avalanche! We were about to be crushed! Then the Secret Shopkin swooped in and rescued us," Apple says.

6

"It all happened so fast, I didn't see who it was," finishes Apple. "I only caught a glimpse of a caped shadow, disappearing into the aisles."

"That. Is. So. Cool!" says Suzie. "Your story is totally going on my Daily Sugar Blog."

"Did somebody say *Secret Shopkin*?" Strawberry Kiss hurries to join her friends.

"Yeah," says Apple. "I was just telling Suzie and Cheeky how he rescued me from a can avalanche."

"I don't believe it!" exclaims Strawberry. "I was saved by the Secret Shopkin, too!"

"It happened yesterday afternoon," Strawberry explains. "I was cleaning off a high shelf when a dust cloud blew up around me. I started coughing. The ladder toppled. And then . . ." She pauses.

"The Secret Shopkin caught me in midair! He zoomed off before I could even say 'thank you.'"

"Wow," says Apple. "I wonder if we'll ever find out who the Secret Shopkin is."

Suddenly, Lippy Lips comes running up. "Guys, come quick!" she cries. "The biggest secret in all of Shopville is about to be unveiled outside the Fashion Boutique!"

Apple gasps. "Could it be?" she asks Strawberry, Suzie, and Cheeky.

Everyone dashes out of Small Mart faster than you can say *quick-rising crust*!

Outside the Fashion Boutique is a huge crowd.

"I guess everybody heard about the secret unveiling," says Apple.

"Of course!" gushes Lippy. "I've been waiting for this all month. I've been practicing just the right shade of surprise to turn."

"You have?" asks Apple.

"Haven't you?" asks Lippy.

"Quick!" Suzie tells Apple. "Let's record this for my blog!"
The friends grab a video camera and start rolling.
"Coming to you fresh from outside the Fashion Boutique,"
Apple announces. "The big moment is finally here!"

00:00:14:07   REC

"That's right," says Suzie. "The answer to the question that totally takes the cake: *Who is the Secret Shopkin?*"

Suddenly, the Fashion Boutique doors open.
A shadowy figure steps out . . .
"Oh my groceries! SHE'S HERE!" cries Lippy.

The shadowy figure is . . .
Shady Diva?

"Hello, darlings!" says Shady.

"*She's* the Secret Shopkin?"
Apple and Suzie gasp.

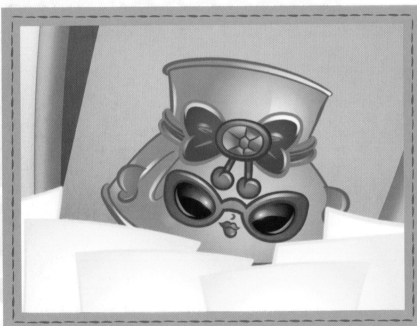

"The secret what?" asks Lippy. "Oh, no, no. She's not the Secret Shopkin. It's even *better*. Today is the day Shady Diva unveils her new *secret* fashion collection!"

"*That's* what you were talking about?" cries Suzie.
"Of course, darlings," says Shady Diva.

Suzie sighs. "Oh, well. I guess the mystery of the Secret Shopkin remains to be solved another day."

00:01:10:16

"But whoever you are," Apple says into the video camera, "we want to thank you. Whenever there's a Shoppie in need, we know the Secret Shopkin will be there."

Meanwhile, back inside Small Mart, it's quiet and empty.
Empty, that is, except for one Shopkin, high on a shelf.
Could it be? Is Kooky the Secret Shopkin?
"Tee-hee-hee," Kooky giggles. "Check ya later!

I ♥ SPK

S

I ♥ SPK